Pearl

THE HAPPY UNICORN

For Imogen Grace. — SALLY ODGERS

For Tammy, Chelsea, Indiana, Tatum, Lenny,
Bandit, Ivy and Basil. — ADELE K THOMAS

Scholastic Press
345 Pacific Highway Lindfield NSW 2070
An imprint of Scholastic Australia Pty Limited (ABN 11 000 614 577)
PO Box 579 Gosford NSW 2250
www.scholastic.com.au

Part of the Scholastic Group
Sydney • Auckland • New York • Toronto • London • Mexico City
• New Delhi • Hong Kong • Buenos Aires • Puerto Rico

Published by Scholastic Australia in 2019.
Text copyright © Sally Odgers, 2019.
Illustrations copyright © Adele K Thomas, 2019.

 A catalogue record for this
NATIONAL book is available from the
LIBRARY National Library of Australia
OF AUSTRALIA

ISBN: 978-1-76066-427-5

The illustrations in this book were created digitally.
Typeset in Queulat Cnd Soft.

Printed in China by RR Donnelley.
Scholastic Australia's policy, in association with RR Donnelley, is to use papers that
are renewable and made efficiently from wood grown in responsibly managed
forests, so as to minimise its environmental footprint.

10 9 8 7 6 5 4 3 2   19 20 21 22 23 / 1

Pearl

Pearl

THE HAPPY UNICORN

SALLY ODGERS ADELE K THOMAS

Chapter One

Pearl the magical unicorn was feeling a little unhappy.

It was raining.

Pearl knew rain was good. It made the plants grow and it meant there was plenty of water in the pond. But did it have to rain so much? Did it have to be so cold? Pearl peered out from under her dripping mane. A big drop of water ran down her horn and splashed into her eye.

'**Bumpy balloons!** Is it ever going to stop?' She swished her tail. Then she shook herself as hard as she could. Drops of water flew from her soggy fur. Then a pink fluffy towel fell out of the sky and landed on Pearl's head.

Pearl was surprised. She'd made just the thing she needed. 'Perfect! Now I have something to keep me dry!' Pearl did a little dance of triumph.

YAY!

But then it started
to rain harder.
Pearl and her pink
towel were soon
soaking wet.

'Tumbling toads!' Pearl
sulked. She shook off the towel and
found a tree. She stood under it, but the
raindrops just slipped off the leaves and
landed on her head.

Pearl wished she had her best friends to talk to.

Her friend Olive was an ogre. And she was probably snug and dry in her ogre-lodge, roasting apples on a stick.

Her friend Tweet was a firebird. She was probably sheltering from the rain in the warm firebird caves.

Pearl couldn't shelter with Olive, because she was far too big to fit in her ogre-lodge.

And she was far too tall to fit into the warm firebird caves with Tweet.

Sometimes being a magical unicorn wasn't so magical.

'I wish I was an ogre,' Pearl muttered. 'They're always happy.'

Then Pearl had an idea. She was a magical unicorn! Maybe she could do a bit of magic to make the rain stop?

'Let's see,' Pearl said. She'd never done this kind of magic before. But how hard could it be? She swished her tail, tapped her front hoof and wiggled. Then she did it again, faster.

Swish-tap-wiggle-swish-tap-wiggle.

Nothing happened, so she added a flick of her mane.

Swish-tap-wiggle-swish-tap-wiggle-flick!

Pearl looked up into the sky. DRIP, DRIP, DRIP, DRIP, DRIP. She snorted crossly. It was still raining, and she was still wet. The only difference was now the rain was pink.

'Rattling roses!' cried Pearl.

She was about to try again when she heard an enormous ROOOAAR!

Then there was another.

ROOOAAR!

Pearl pricked up her ears and flicked
pink rain off her mane.

That sounded like Olive.
What was Olive doing
out in the rain?

Pearl trotted off to
find out what was
going on.

Olive was on the other side of the pond.
Pearl watched as the ogre clenched
her fists, stomped one ogre-foot on the
ground and roared.

A twitter of giggles came from a huge hat sitting on a rock nearby.

Her friend Tweet the firebird stuck her beak out from underneath. 'Pearl!' she said excitedly.

Olive looked around with a grin.
She flung her arms around Pearl in
a squelchy, wet hug. 'Did you make
the pink rain?'

'Happy rain,' Tweet said, flapping
her wings.

Pearl didn't tell her friends she was trying to make the rain stop. Then Pearl no longer felt the DRIP, DRIP, DRIP of raindrops. The rain had stopped! Pearl felt happier already.

'What are you doing?' Pearl asked.

'Ogre-roar!' Tweet said. The firebird came out from under the hat, stomped one claw and stuck out her tail.

'I'm practising for the roar contest at Ogrefest. It's going to be so much fun,' Olive said.

Pearl wished she had a Unicornfest to go to, but she was the only unicorn in the Kingdom, so it wouldn't be much fun at all.

'I'm going to enter lots of contests. There's the ogre-stomp, the cake-eat, the campfire, the mud-roll . . .'

'The mud-roll?' Pearl asked. 'That sounds like fun.'

'We roll around in mud and then we shake it off. I'll show you.'

Olive flung herself down and rolled across the ground. Then she bounced back to her feet, dripping with mud.

'Now we shake.' She shook herself and mud splattered all over Pearl.

'Oops,' Olive said. 'You don't look like a magical unicorn anymore.'

Pearl shook the mud off and managed to splatter Tweet. 'Oops.'

'Ogrecorn and ogrebird!' Tweet giggled.

'I know!' Olive clapped her hands. 'Let's ALL go to Ogrefest!'

Chapter Two

Pearl couldn't wait to go to Ogrefest! But there was just one problem . . .

'Olive, we aren't ogres,' Pearl said.
'Only ogres can go to Ogrefest.'

'Not green,' Tweet agreed, flicking mud
off her orange crest.

'That's easy to fix. We'll use Granny
Ogma's ogre-lotion! Wait here.'

Olive picked an armful of big green leaves from a nearby bush. She put them in the huge hat and scooped lots of mud on top.

Pearl and Tweet looked at each other worriedly.

'**Fizzing fish**, Olive, you're not going to eat that are you?' Pearl said.

Ogres eat almost anything, but this was going too far, even for Olive.

Olive laughed. 'Watch.' She put the hat full of leaves and mud on the ground and jumped in with both feet. Then she started stomping.

Slosh, slosh, squelch, squelch, stomp, stomp went Olive.

For a while, the stuff in the huge hat was just a mix of mud and bits of green leaf, but slowly it turned a strong shade of green.

'There!' Olive said proudly.

'Green mud!' Tweet laughed.

'My granny, Ogma the Bold, makes this for ogres who feel a bit off-colour. Now, hold still. I'm going to turn you into ogres!'

Pearl really wanted to go to Ogrefest. She wanted to have fun and be happy like an ogre.

Olive scooped up the green mud and rubbed it into Pearl's white fur.

'Perfect,' she said.

Pearl trotted over to the pond and peered in. Her green and pink reflection peered back. **Tap-dancing turnips!** Olive was right. She didn't look like Pearl the magical unicorn anymore. She looked like Pearl, the ogre unicorn.

While Pearl was looking at herself, Tweet hopped into the huge hat and flapped about in the green mud. Then she hopped out and strutted about with her feathers dripping in green goo. 'Ogrebird,' she growled.

RARR!

Olive clapped her hands. 'You need some horns.'

She picked up some short sticks and stuck them to Pearl and Tweet.

'What about my real horn?' Pearl asked.

'Flowers,' Tweet said.

Olive picked pink dandelions and wild roses and made them into a flower crown. She fitted it snugly over Pearl's horn. Olive made flower crowns for herself and Tweet as well.

'Now we look like sisters,' Olive said.

Pearl wasn't sure about that, but Olive was so happy that she decided to be happy too.

'Now, I'm going to teach you how to be ogres,' Olive said. 'You have to roar, and stomp, and eat a lot, and have lots and lots of fun.'

That sounded easy, but Pearl still wasn't sure. 'Tweet and I can't roar.'

'No,' said Olive. 'But, you will be really good at the ogre-stomp contest! You sing and stomp your feet like this.' Olive stomped her feet and started to sing.

'Stomp, stomp, ogre stomp!
Stompety, stompety, stomp-stomp!
Munch, munch, all your lunch!
Munch and crunch your lunchety lunch!
Stompety, stompety, stomp-stomp!'

Pearl copied Olive. She stomped as
hard as she could with her four hooves.
It was so much fun! And she could get
in some extra stomps with her two
extra feet.

Olive and Tweet cheered.

'Me?' Tweet asked.

'You'll be great at the campfire contest, Tweet,' Olive said. 'All you have to do is gather sticks and make a fire.'

'Easy peasy!' Tweet zipped about, picking up twigs. When she had enough, she dropped them in a pile and flicked her tail to make a fire.

Pearl laughed. This was going to work!
It really was. She was going to be an
ogre! And ogres were always happy.

Stompety, stompety, stomp-stomp-
stomp, went Pearl. She added a swish
of her tail and a flick of her mane, just
for fun.

A big pink cake fell with a PLOP into the huge hat. Olive gave a yell of delight, grabbed the cake, and took a big bite. It was covered in green mud. 'Want some?' she mumbled.

YUMMY!

Pearl and Tweet shook their heads.

Olive finished the cake and licked her fingers. 'Pearl! That was delicious, but remember, ogres don't do magic.'

'I'll be careful,' Pearl promised. She was going to try her very best to be an ogre.

Chapter Three

Ogrefest was held at Bigmouth Ogre Lake Valley.

All the ogres from Olive's tribe stomped along to the valley, roaring songs and eating snacks. They carried more snacks piled high on wooden carts.

'Those are for the eating contest,' Olive told Tweet and Pearl. 'I hope the other tribes bring lots of snacks too. I could eat a whole pumpkin and five apples and a honeycomb and–'

'Hungry,' Tweet squawked. She flew down and clung to Pearl's mane, pointing at all the food.

'I could eat two dozen eggs and fifteen pancakes,' Olive continued.

Now Pearl was getting hungry too. She was just about to make snacks for them all when she remembered. She mustn't do any magic. Otherwise the ogres would know she wasn't really an ogre.

As they stomped into the valley, an enormous ogre greeted them with a roar! He had the biggest ogre-horns Pearl had ever seen.

'That's Boris the Brave,' Olive explained.

ROARR!

Then they heard another, even bigger roar as two other tribes of ogres stomped into the valley. Everyone stomped, shook their fists and roared as they danced around the lake.

It sounded loud and scary, but suddenly the roars changed to laughter, and the ogres hugged one another happily.

Olive hugged Pearl, and Tweet stomped up and down on Pearl's back.

RAARR!

The first contest of the day was the great ogre-boat contest. Teams of ogres carried planks of wood and rope to the shores of the lake.

Pearl, Olive and Tweet made their own team. Pearl and Olive dragged the wood to the shore and Tweet flew overhead with rope in her beak. It was fun, but Tweet wasn't strong enough to move planks and Pearl found her hooves weren't nearly as useful as Olive's hands.

'**Pink parakeets!** This would be easier if I could do magic,' Pearl grumbled.

Olive laughed. 'Ogres don't do magic,' she reminded her. 'Only Pearl the magical unicorn can do that.'

When the ogre-boats were built, the teams paddled them across the lake. The first team across won medals and an apple pie the size of a wheelbarrow!

Pearl's mouth watered. She loved apple pie. But because she had hooves and Tweet had wings, their team came last.

'Don't worry,' said Olive. 'There are plenty more contests!'

Luckily, the winning ogres shared their big apple pie with everyone who entered.

'Yum!' Tweet mumbled through a beak full of pie. She saw a large ogre staring at her.

'You're small for an ogre,' the ogre said.

'Ogrebird!' Tweet stomped her claws on the ground.

RAARR!

The ogre grinned and gave Tweet another piece of pie.

Next, Pearl and Tweet went to watch Olive in the cake-eating contest. They chanted, 'Eat! Eat! Eat!' along with the rest of the ogres.

Olive ate seven cakes in two minutes, but another ogre ate eight. Olive came second!

She beamed as Boris the Brave put a silver medal around her neck.

'Go, Olive!' Pearl and Tweet cheered.

Chapter Four

Soon it was time for the ogre-stomp contest. Pearl was nervous.

'I don't know about this,' Pearl said.

'You can do it, Pearl!' Olive said. 'Tweet and I will cheer for you.'

Pearl walked into the ogre-stomp area. Then the audience started to clap and an ogre-band started to play.

'Stomp, stomp, ogre stomp!
Stompety, stompety, stomp-stomp!'

Pearl stomped and stomped. She pranced and bounced. Her hooves hit the ground in time with the music. It was the best fun ever! She swished her tail and wiggled her head.

Slowly the other ogres dancing the ogre-stomp started to get tired.

'Munch, munch, all your lunch!
Munch and crunch your lunchety lunch!'

Pearl heard Olive's voice roaring above the others. Olive wore the biggest ogre grin Pearl had ever seen.

GO PEARL!

Soon there were just three contestants left. Pearl felt as if she could go on forever! Stomp! Stomp! Swish-wiggle-shake! Shake, shimmy-shimmy-toss-wiggle . . . Oops! Pearl stopped stomping. She had almost done magic!

Because she stopped stomping, Pearl was out of the contest.

Olive and Tweet hugged her.

'You were great!' said Olive.

'Stomp! Stomp!' said Tweet.

The crowd laughed and cheered for the winner of the ogre-stomp.

Tweet's campfire contest was next.
Pearl watched excitedly as her tiny
friend zipped around and gathered twigs.
Then when she had a pile, Tweet lit her
fire with a sweep of her firebird tail.

Pearl thought Tweet's fire was the nicest, but some ogres made huge fires and others started roasting apples.

Boris the Brave said anything with added apples had to be the winner.

'Well done, Tweet!' said Pearl.

Olive entered the ogre-roar contest
next. She almost won but an ogre-baby
roared so loudly, everyone had to cover
their ears.

'Winner!' Boris the Brave yelled.

RAAAAAARRR!

Then Olive entered the sniffing contest. She was blindfolded and had to guess the items after sniffing them. Pearl watched Olive sniff out a dirty sock, a caramel pie, a marshmallow, a small fish, six toffees and a bottle of milk.

Pearl twitched her ear, because it tickled. Then she flicked her tail twice and tossed her mane. Twitch-flick-flick-toss!

Oops! Oh no! A cloud of pink butterflies fluttered down from the sky and settled on the heads of the ogres sitting next to her. They looked up at the butterflies, surprised.

Pearl was about to apologise but before she could say anything there was a loud screeching and squealing noise from the hillside.

Pearl looked up and saw a group of gobble-uns running down the hill, heading straight for Ogrefest!

Chapter Five

Pearl had **never** seen so many gobble-uns before!

Usually, they went about in groups of three or four, because they didn't like one another very much.

Today there were dozens of them, yelling and squealing in their high, scratchy gobble-un voices. They tore through the valley with their long twitchy fingers and their dirty ears.

'Boats! Sink 'em!' howled one of the gobble-uns. He was one of the biggest gobble-uns Pearl had ever seen.

STOMP!   SMASH!

Three of the gobble-uns had clubs. They swung them hard and hit the ogre-boats everyone had worked so hard to build.

The gobble-uns tossed what was left of the boats into the campfires, and squashed all the apples, that were meant for roasting, with their feet.

Olive was still wearing her blindfold. She spun around at the noise.

Tweet flew up and pecked the knot of the blindfold until it fell off.

Olive blinked and stared. 'What's going on, Pearl?'

'Gobble-uns,' Pearl said.

A loud howl rose into the air as the
gobble-uns found the snack carts.
They grabbed the snacks and started
throwing them onto the ground.

'What are they doing?' Olive cried.
'Food is for eating, not for throwing
. . . unless it's a food-throwing
competition, of course, and then we
always catch it in our mouths.'

'Wash it?' Tweet suggested.

PLONK!

Boris the Brave stomped over to the gobble-uns. 'Get out!' he roared.

'Why should we?' sneered one of the gobble-uns.

'Ogrefest is for having fun!' said Olive.

'Gobble-uns know how to have fun! Watch this.' The gobble-un wiggled his filthy fingers and a wave of stinky magic flew through the air.

Chapter Six

The smell was horrible. Pearl could hardly breathe.

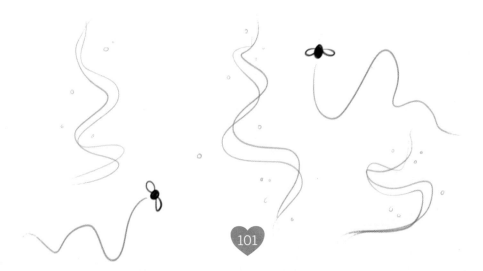

All the ogres at Ogrefest were coughing and sneezing. Even Boris the Brave spluttered on the ground. Then Pearl realised what was happening. Ogre-noses were sensitive. Olive could sniff the difference between a red apple and a green one. The horrible stinky magic must have been worse for ogres than for unicorns or firebirds.

AH CHoo!

The gobble-uns howled with laughter.
'Everyone knows ogres are weak.
A bit of stinky magic and they
fall right over. Ha! Ha! Ha!'

Rotten radishes! Pearl had never been so angry in her life. *Right,* she thought. She wasn't an ogre. She was a magical unicorn. Pearl stamped her hoof. She swished her tail angrily. Then she spun around and kicked both hind legs in the air.

'That doesn't look like an ogre,' said one of the gobble-uns.

She thought about a windstorm, roaring through Bigmouth Ogre Lake Valley.

Jumping jellypots! She could fix this.

Swish-tap-wiggle-swish-tap-wiggle-flick! went Pearl.

SWOOSH! Down came the magic pink rain.

The pink rain poured down, wetting the gobble-uns, making them clean. The gobble-uns shrieked with anger and started running away up the hillside.

The stinky magic quickly disappeared. The ogres got up and stomped after the gobble-uns, roaring loudly.

Pearl, Olive and Tweet giggled as they watched.

Chapter Seven

When the ogres returned, they were grinning from ear to ear.

The pink rain continued to pour down, wetting Pearl, her friends and the ogres. Pearl smiled. Why had she thought rain was a bad thing? Though now she wasn't quite sure how to make it stop.

'Campfire!' Tweet squawked.

'Ogre-roast!' Olive roared.

'Campfire! Ogre-roast!' the ogres chanted.

When the rain finally stopped, Tweet used her firebird flames to get the campfire burning. The pink rain had cleaned the muddy food, and soon everyone was roasting apples on sticks and roaring ogre-songs.

'Munch, munch, all your lunch!
Munch and crunch your lunchety lunch!'

Pearl was delighted. Her magic had worked, and Ogrefest was just as much fun as she thought it would be. She looked around the campfire at the green ogres waving their apples and singing. Then she looked at Tweet, whose feathers glowed firebird orange. Then she looked down at herself.

UH-OH!

She and Tweet were clean! Her magic rain had washed away the green ogre-lotion.

'**Flittering flapjacks**, Olive, I'm Pearl the magical unicorn again!'

Her voice was much louder than she meant it to be.

Oh no.

The ogres stopped munching and crunching. They looked at Pearl and then at Tweet.

Pearl stumbled to her feet. 'S-sorry,' she said.

Then Boris the Brave grinned at her. 'What for?'

'Not ogrebird,' Tweet squawked sadly. 'Firebird really.'

'And I'm not really an ogre unicorn,' Pearl said.

There was a pause around the campfire. Then Boris the Brave laughed until he nearly fell over. 'We can see that now!' he roared.

'You might not be real ogres, but you are a lot like ogres.'

'You're brave! You stood up to the gobble-uns,' an ogre yelled from the other side of the fire.

'You're clever. You got rid of them,' another one said.

'You're kind. You cheered for Olive in all of the contests,' an older ogre said.

'So let's feast!' Boris the Brave roared.

Pearl, Olive and Tweet were about to start eating when suddenly it started raining again! Their campfire went out. It was cold, wet and sploshy.

'Can you fix this, Pearl?' Olive asked.

'I can try.' She was so happy to be a magical unicorn again.

Swish-tap-wiggle-swish-tap-wiggle-flick! went Pearl.

The rain stopped. Pearl smiled. Then suddenly plops of pink yoghurt fell from the sky. PLOP, PLOP, PLOP, PLOP, PLOP!

'Bothering bats!' Pearl said.

But all the ogres roared with delight
and opened their mouths. They danced
about, trying to catch every delicious,
yoghurty drop.

Pearl pranced with delight. Being
an ogre was fun, but being a magical
unicorn was even better!

MORE MAGICAL ADVENTURES COMING SOON!

Pearl

THE BRAVE UNICORN

SALLY ODGERS   ADELE K THOMAS

PeaRL